SHOW AND TELL

SHOW
AND
TELL

by
Stephanie Greene

illustrated by
Elaine Clayton

Clarion Books/New York

Clarion Books
a Houghton Mifflin Company imprint
215 Park Avenue South, New York, NY 10003
Text copyright © 1998 by Stephanie Greene
Illustrations copyright © 1998 by Elaine Clayton

The text is 15.5/18.5 Granjon.
The illustrations for this book were executed
in pen and ink with ink wash.

Printed in the USA.

Library of Congress Cataloging-in-Publication Data
Greene, Stephanie.
Show and tell / by Stephanie Greene ; illustrated
by Elaine Clayton
p.   cm.
Summary: Second grader Woody is having trouble
with Miss Plunkett, the new student teacher who
doesn't like his show-and-tell, and with Ethan, the
kid who lives across the street.
ISBN 0-395-88898-0
[1. Teacher-student relationships—Fiction. 2. Friendships—
Fiction. 3. Schools—Fiction. 4. Show-and-tell presentations—
Fiction.] I. Clayton, Elaine, ill. II. Title.
PZ7.G8438Sh   1998
[Fic]—dc21   98-10814
CIP
AC

MV 10 9 8 7 6 5 4 3 2 1

For Oliver,
and in memory of the real Huey
—S.G.

To my former teaching partner,
Peter Thorlichen
—E.C.

Contents

1.

Belly-Up

Huey was floating at the top of the tank. Belly-up.

"Is he dead?"

Woody knelt down next to his aquarium. "I think so," he said. "Fish don't usually swim upside down."

Ethan knelt beside him. "My dad says parrots die with their eyes open." He pushed his nose up against the glass. "His eyes are definitely open."

"Fish don't have eyelids," Woody said. He rubbed at Ethan's greasy nose spot with his sleeve. "But he's dead all right. He's been getting smaller and smaller all week."

Huey's pale blue body bobbed peacefully up and down. The other fish were darting all around it. It looked as if they were playing tag.

Woody took a green net out of a drawer. "He used to be the same size as Pinky."

"Who's Pinky?" said Ethan.

"That one over there. She's his wife." He pointed to a fat little pink fish. "Huey's a blueberry tetra and Pinky's a strawberry tetra."

Woody knew the common names of all his fish. Every time he got a new fish, he looked it up in a fish book. Then he wrote its name down in his special fish notebook.

When one died, he wrote "deceased."

That meant dead.

Woody had learned that fish died quite often when you had an aquarium. Keeping fish was much harder than he'd expected. He tried to be very careful. But fish still died.

It didn't hurt as much anymore. But he still

liked the sound of "deceased" better than "dead."

"She doesn't look very sad," Ethan said. "Maybe they were divorced."

"Fish don't get divorced," said Woody. "Once they're married, that's it."

"Who says?" Ethan said. "Anyway, how do you know which one is the boy?"

"I just know, that's all." Actually, Woody didn't know. But he wasn't about to tell Ethan that.

Ethan thought he knew everything, just because his dad was a scientist. He was always bragging about his dad, even though he didn't live with him.

Woody didn't know how great a dad he could be if he didn't even live with his own son.

Ethan wasn't even really Woody's friend. He had moved in across the street with his mom and baby brother right before school started. His mom worked, so Ethan came over every day after school to wait until she picked up the baby from daycare and got home.

"Why can't he wait in his own house?" Woody had asked his mom at breakfast one morning. "Why do I have to have him over?"

"I can't let a child of seven stay all by himself when we're here," Woody's mom said. She put a glass of milk in front of him. "He'll be lonely."

"I don't even like him," Woody said. "Why can't he go to after-school?"

"I don't think St. Joseph's has after-school."

"What about a baby sitter?"

"Hey." Woody's dad sat down on the other side of the table. "Aren't you being a little mean?" He didn't sound mad, he sounded disappointed. Woody looked down. "Give him a chance."

Woody could feel his dad looking at him. His dad was nice to everyone. "He never wants to do anything," Woody said into his lap.

"I think he's shy," his mom said. "You've got good ideas. I bet you can interest him in something."

So Woody tried. But every time he suggested something, Ethan shrugged and said, "I don't care."

Sometimes he followed Woody around and watched what he was doing. Mostly, he sat on the couch and looked out the window at his house. Then the minute his mom's car pulled into his driveway, he ran across the street.

He never even said good-bye.

"That's rude," Woody had said hotly. "If I did that, you'd yell."

"You're right," Mrs. Baldwin said. "I'll yell at Ethan when I've known him longer. Does that make you feel better?"

It didn't. Woody still hated having someone around every afternoon. He liked to be alone. He liked to talk to his fish in his head. He liked to build forts and play both the good guys and the bad guys. He liked to put on different voices and yell out loud.

He couldn't do any of that with Ethan watching.

Woody wished Ethan's mother would pull into the driveway right now. He took the lid off the fish tank.

"What are you doing?" Ethan said.

Woody lowered the net into the water. "I have to get him out before the other fish eat him."

"Gross," said Ethan. "They eat their friends?"

Woody scooped up Huey's body and took the dripping net to his desk. He turned it over. Huey plopped out.

Seeing the tiny body out of water gave Woody a funny, tight feeling in his throat. He picked Huey up and cradled him in his hand.

"You can barely feel him," he said. He moved his hand up and down in the air. "He doesn't even weigh one ounce, I bet. But he has a heart and a stomach and everything. It's amazing."

"That's nothing," Ethan said. "My dad says there are animals with all that stuff who could fit on the head of a pin. That's more amazing."

Woody ignored him. He ran his finger down Huey's side.

"You shouldn't touch that thing," said Ethan. "That guy's covered with germs."

"He is not," Woody said indignantly. "He's beautiful."

"You have to flush him down the toilet. That's what people do with dead fish."

"No way," Woody said. "That would be like you flushing Gordon down the toilet."

"Gordon's my brother. You don't flush brothers down the toilet."

"Well, Huey's like my brother."

Ethan pinched his nostrils closed. "You better do something quick. He stinks."

That was it. Huey was dead, and now some kid who'd never even known him was being mean to him.

Woody thought a person had to be pretty terrible to insult a dead fish.

"Oh, yeah?" Woody spun around and Ethan jumped back. He dangled Huey's body in front of Ethan's face. "Then maybe you'd better eat him now."

"You're crazy," Ethan shouted. "I'm getting out of here." He turned and headed for the stairs. "You'll probably die of fish germs," he yelled from the bottom.

Woody heard the kitchen door slam. He put

Huey gently on the table. *I wouldn't really let him eat you,* he thought to Huey. *Don't worry.*

He opened the little red heart-shaped box his mom had given him after she ate the candy inside. He took out the sharks' teeth from Florida and the arrowhead he had found in the stream.

Then he laid Huey gently inside.

When Huey did start to smell, Woody bet he'd smell like blueberries.

He had tried saving fish that died when he first got his tank. His mom had practically fainted when she discovered them in a bag in his underwear drawer. So he knew he had to get rid of Huey before then.

But not yet.

First, there was something he had to do. He had to show Huey to Mrs. Carver. She was his favorite teacher ever. She knew how much he loved fish. He wrote about them in his journal. He drew pictures of them in art.

Woody knew she'd love Huey, dead or alive.

He could hardly wait for show and tell.

2.

I Have a Surprise for You

"**B**oys and girls?"

Woody heard Mrs. Carver's voice.

He hunched over his paper. His picture was almost done.

"Boys and girls."

This time it was an order.

Woody looked up with his pencil frozen in midair.

Mrs. Carver was looking right at him. Without moving his eyes, Woody lowered his pencil to the desk. Her eyes moved on.

"I want to see all eyes on me." She swept the

whole room with her gaze. Her head turned from one side to the other and back again.

Mrs. Carver's look always reminded Woody of a searchlight. Like the one that swept through the sky near the airport at night.

She didn't yell, she looked. And she waited.

One by one, all the kids stopped what they were doing.

It worked every time.

"I have a surprise for you," she said now. Her voice didn't sound as if something they would like was about to happen, Woody thought. It sounded as if something they wouldn't like had already happened. And there was nothing they could do about it.

He frowned.

She turned around and held out her arm. "This is Miss Plunkett."

A shortish, roundish woman Woody hadn't noticed raised her hand and wiggled her fingers at them. She had on a huge flowered dress that looked like a tent. She had a ring on almost every finger. Her nails and lips were bright red.

Woody had never seen such perfect lips. They looked like Mr. Potato Head lips.

"Miss Plunkett is going to be our student teacher for a while," Mrs. Carver said. "She got here earlier than I expected, so I haven't had time to tell you about her. But I know we're all going to enjoy having her in our class."

Oh no we're not, Woody thought. He hated student teachers. They never knew anyone's name. They didn't know how anything worked.

They changed everything.

Woody didn't like it when things changed. He loved having Mrs. Carver and no one else.

Someone poked him in the ribs. It was Billy Bart. He sat next to Woody because both their last names started with B.

All the kids called Billy the Time-out King because he was there so much. He couldn't sit still. He was always making jokes and acting silly.

He made Woody laugh even when Woody knew he shouldn't.

On the first day of school, Billy had said to him, "Want to be my best friend?" Just like that.

Woody didn't know what to say. He wanted a best friend. Everyone in second grade did. Having a best friend meant you had someone to sit with at lunch. And play with at recess.

But once you picked a best friend, you weren't supposed to change. And after only one day, Woody wasn't sure he wanted his to be Billy.

So he said, "I have to sleep on it," the way his dad did when he was thinking of saying no.

Billy asked him practically every day, but Woody still hadn't made up his mind.

Now Billy pointed to Miss Plunkett and puffed out his cheeks. Meaning she was fat.

Woody looked at the other kids. Franklin was poking Brad with his ruler. Lisa was whispering behind her hand to Lynn and Katie.

The only one paying attention was Brianna. She was sitting up straight with her hands folded in front of her. She was moving them

around in the air above her desk so Miss Plunkett would notice them.

So Miss Plunkett would know how polite she was.

Woody felt the ends of his mouth turn down.

"I've told Miss Plunkett what a good group of children you are," Mrs. Carver was saying. "And she's looking forward to getting to know you. Aren't you, Miss Plunkett?"

"Yes, I am." Miss Plunkett gave a funny nervous cough. Woody saw a red splotch on her neck. "I'm very excited about being here. I hope we're going to become good friends."

No one said anything for a minute. They were all watching her perfect lips move.

Mrs. Carver said, "Class, say hello to Miss Plunkett."

"Hello, Miss Plunkett," they said in one voice.

"I know you're going to be on your best behavior so you can show Miss Plunkett what wonderful boys and girls you are," Mrs. Carver said. "Are there any questions?"

Lynn's hand shot up in the air.

"Yes, Lynn?"

"Are those lips real?"

Some of the kids giggled. Brianna frowned to show Lynn she wasn't being polite.

"Lynn." Mrs. Carver pursed her lips. She shook her head no.

"That's all right," said Miss Plunkett. She smiled, but the splotch on her neck was bigger. "Yes, they are."

Lynn opened her mouth to say more.

"That's enough." Mrs. Carver said in a firm voice. The phone behind her desk rang. She went to pick it up.

Everyone was staring at Miss Plunkett. Lynn leaned forward over her desk. "How do you eat with those lips?" she whispered.

Miss Plunkett leaned forward, too. "Very carefully," she said in a loud whisper. She winked and Lynn smiled.

Mrs. Carver hung up the phone. "I have to go to the principal's office for a minute, so I'm going to ask Miss Plunkett to do show and tell with you. Everyone who has something to show, go and get it from your cubby. The rest of you can clean your desks and sit in circle."

She and Miss Plunkett started to talk in low voices.

Some of the kids rushed to the cubbies. Woody put his paper in his desk.

He didn't want to show Huey to Miss Plunkett. He wanted to wait for Mrs. Carver.

But if he waited, Huey might start to smell. He knew he had to do it today.

He dragged his feet to his cubby. He could tell Lynn liked Miss Plunkett. He knew all the girls would like her because she wore lipstick and nail polish.

But not him. Not after the student teacher last year.

Her name was Miss Dodd. She made them sit with their noses touching their desks for ten minutes when they were bad.

Not their heads, their noses.

It was a lot harder.

When they went to lunch, she made them line up in two lines, then hold hands with the person next to them. It was usually someone they hated.

If Miss Plunkett lined him up next to Brianna, he wouldn't eat. He didn't care if he starved.

Woody got his box and sat down on the floor as far away from Miss Plunkett as he could.

"When I get back, I know Miss Plunkett is going to tell me how good you were," Mrs. Carver said to them. Then, before anyone could even say good-bye, she went out and shut the door.

Woody stared at the closed door. He couldn't believe it.

Mrs. Carver had left them.

They were all alone with a total stranger.

3.

Huey Meets Miss Plunkett

"**W**ho would like to go first?" Miss Plunkett said. She sat down in Mrs. Carver's rocking chair and looked around the circle. The girls slid sideways to be closer. They were almost on her feet.

Brianna's hand shot up. "Oh. Oh. Oh. Oh." She jiggled up and down on her bottom.

"What's your name?" said Miss Plunkett.

Brianna tilted her head to one side so that her long blond hair would fall over one cheek. "Brianna."

"All right, Brianna. What do you have to show today?"

Brianna stood up with her paper bag. "My father went on a business trip to Arizona," she said. "He's very important and he was very busy, but he still had time to buy me this."

She reached in and pulled out an Indian doll. It had a beaded headband and long brown hair and a skirt with fringe.

All the girls gasped.

"No one can touch it because it's very expensive," Brianna said. "It's made out of porcelain."

The girls were leaning forward. Every time one of them stretched out her hand, Brianna hugged the doll to her chest and frowned.

"It's beautiful," said Miss Plunkett. "Can you tell the boys and girls what porcelain is?"

"It's like china," said Brianna.

"How much did it cost?" asked Billy.

"It's not polite to ask what something cost," Miss Plunkett told him.

"Fifty dollars," Brianna said quickly.

"Wow." They were all impressed.

Billy always wanted to know what everything

cost, Woody thought. And Brianna always wanted to tell.

Everyone knew that except Miss Plunkett.

Miss Plunkett sat up straight and smoothed her dress over her knees. "All right, Brianna, that's fine. You can sit down now."

She looked around the circle. "Who would like to go next?"

More hands shot up. Miss Plunkett pointed to Andrew. "Tell me your name and then show the class what you have."

"My name is Andrew White. I threw up last night."

"Oh. That's too bad, Andrew." Miss Plunkett sounded surprised. "Maybe you should sit down."

"You could see everything," Andrew said. "The corn was still in perfect kernels."

"All right, Andrew, that's enough."

"But the peas was just green, runny stuff."

"Andrew." Miss Plunkett stood up so quickly that the hem of her huge flowered dress swept over Lynn's head. "I said, sit down, please."

Andrew sat down.

Billy was holding his neck and making gagging noises. Brianna held her stomach and made a face. "He's disgusting, isn't he, Miss Plunkett?"

Lynn was still under Miss Plunkett's dress. All they could see were her hands folded in her lap. She seemed to be frozen. Woody thought she was probably dead. If it was him, he would be. Dead of embarrassment.

It was so weird, no one even laughed.

He saw Lynn's hand reach up and tug at the hem of Miss Plunkett's dress.

"Miss Plunkett?" He could barely hear her.

Miss Plunkett looked down. "Oh, dear, I'm so sorry." She swept her dress away from Lynn's head. Lynn's face was bright red. Her hair was standing up on one side from electricity.

"Oh, dear," Miss Plunkett said again. She bent down and tried to smooth Lynn's hair. "Oh, my."

"That's okay," Lynn said. She looked more embarrassed than Miss Plunkett.

"Well. That was kind of silly." Miss Plunkett smiled at them as if she were waiting for someone to say something.

No one did.

"Okay," she said in a bright voice. "Let's start again, shall we?" She sat down and rocked from side to side, tucking her dress under her.

Everyone was still staring at her.

"Now." She patted her hair all over as if she was putting out a fire. "Does anyone else have something they'd like to show the class?"

The silence was so loud, it made Woody nervous. He crept his hand along the side of his face as high as his ear. He hunched his shoulders.

"Wonderful," Miss Plunkett said. "What's your name?"

"Woody."

"What do you have to show today, Woody?"

"My fish."

"Oh, how nice." Miss Plunkett sounded relieved. "I'm sure we'd all love to see your fish. Stand up so everyone can see."

Woody stood up and put his hand in his pocket.

"Did you bring him in a bowl?" said Miss Plunkett.

"He doesn't need a bowl," said Woody. He took out his little box. "I have him in this box."

"But that's not good for a fish, Woody," said Miss Plunkett. "He needs water."

"No, he doesn't," Woody said. He opened the box and took Huey out by the tail.

He held him up in the air.

"This is Huey. He's dead."

4.

Miss Plunkett Stinks

Woody was tracing patterns in the dust on the floor of the hall when Mrs. Carver got back. He didn't know she was there until he saw her feet in front of him.

He didn't look up.

"Woody Baldwin. What are you doing out here?"

Woody could hear the surprise in her voice. He crossed his arms and tucked his hands into his armpits.

Mrs. Carver knelt down beside him. She put her hand on top of his head.

"Woody?"

He looked up.

"What happened? I've never had to send you out to the hall."

Her dark blue eyes looked so kind, it made his lower lip quiver. He squeezed his mouth as tight as he could.

"Oh, dear." Mrs. Carver rubbed her hand in circles on his back. "Tell me what happened."

"She took Huey," Woody said.

"Who did?"

"Miss Plunkett."

"Oh," said Mrs. Carver. "Who's Huey?"

"My fish. I had him for show and tell."

"Oh, I see," Mrs. Carver said. "Well, maybe Miss Plunkett didn't want him to get hurt, Woody. Did she put him up on the shelf?"

"No. She threw him in the garbage."

"The garbage? Why would Miss Plunkett throw your fish in the garbage?"

Woody felt a lump in his throat. "She said he had germs. She said he would make everyone sick. She made me give him to her."

Mrs. Carver's face went fuzzy.

"Then she threw him in the garbage."

"I'm confused." Mrs. Carver tapped her upper lip with her pointer finger. Woody wiped his eyes with the back of his hand.

Mrs. Carver looked right into his eyes. "And what did you do to get sent out here?"

Woody sniffed. "I told her she stinks."

"Oh, Woody." She stood up. "It wasn't right to tell her that. She's an adult and I left her in charge."

Woody looked back down at the dusty floor. He heard Mrs. Carver sigh.

"You can't tell someone they stink just because they do something you don't like." He could tell she wasn't feeling sorry for him anymore. "Let me talk to Miss Plunkett about this."

She went into the room and shut the door. Woody drew his legs up to his chest and rested his forehead on his knees.

Mrs. Carver used to be his friend. She'd given him the "Good Citizen" award last month. Now she was mad at him.

He was right about Miss Plunkett changing everything.

It was already starting.

• • •

When the door opened again, Woody looked up. It was Miss Plunkett.

He put his head back down on his knees.

All she said was, "Woody?" She didn't kneel down like Mrs. Carver. She stood way above him, like she was the boss.

"I'm sorry about your fish," she said. "I like animals, but not dead ones. Most people don't."

Woody didn't say anything.

"They're dirty and usually diseased and I don't think people should handle them," said Miss Plunkett. "It's not healthy."

Woody looked at her. "What about hamburgers?"

"Excuse me?"

"Hamburgers are dead animals," he said. "And chicken. I bet you touch chicken."

"It's not the same thing."

"My dad lets me hold dead fish. He lets me watch while he cleans them. I get to see their insides and everything. He doesn't care about germs."

Thinking about his dad made his lower lip start to tremble again. He pressed his lips together.

"Look, Woody, I don't want to argue with you," Miss Plunkett said. "I want us to have a good time together."

She held out his box. "Put this in your cubby and don't bring it out until it's time to go home, okay?"

She held open the door. "Mrs. Carver said you should come in and start reading."

Woody slid past her. He didn't say "Okay" and he didn't say "Thank you." He went over to his cubby and knelt down.

He opened the box.

There was Huey, covered with little bits of the glitter they had used in art.

Woody longed to wipe him off, but he didn't dare.

He closed the lid and put the box under his backpack.

Miss Plunkett didn't have to tell him not to bring it out. He wasn't going to show her anything he cared about, ever again.

It was only her first day. But Woody could hardly wait until it was her last.

5.

"Good-bye and Good Luck"

"**W**hat are you doing?"

Ethan was standing behind him. The sun was shining through his bristly hair. Woody could see his white scalp underneath.

"Planting." Woody put down his trowel and opened up his box. He picked up Huey for the last time. "Good-bye and good luck," he said.

He dropped the little blue body into the hole.

"Good luck? What kind of good luck can he have?" said Ethan. "He's dead."

Woody ignored him. This was the part when he liked to be alone.

It made him remember an old movie he had watched with his mom and dad. A mother and father had to say good-bye to their son at the train station. He was going to fight in a war. He might get killed and they would never see him again.

The father was trying to be brave, so all he said was, "Good-bye and good luck."

The son came home at the end, but Woody had never forgotten how sad it was to let him go.

Dropping Huey into the hole was definitely the hardest part of having him die.

Even without Ethan standing there, watching.

Woody opened the seed packet he'd found in the kitchen drawer. He took out some seeds and dropped them into the hole on top of Huey.

Then he started to fill up the hole with soil.

Ethan watched for a while. "I know what you're doing," he said suddenly. "You're using him for fertilizer, like the Indians showed the Pilgrims."

Woody didn't say anything. He patted down the soil.

"I think they used big fish from the ocean," Ethan said. "That guy's not going to produce very much fertilizer."

"I already know that," said Woody. He smoothed the soil and stuck a stick in the ground to mark the spot.

"Hey, I have an idea." Ethan squatted down next to him. His face was so close, Woody could see a faint line of freckles running up and over his nose.

It looked like ants marching.

"What?" said Woody.

"We can do an experiment," said Ethan. "Like my dad."

"What kind of experiment?" said Woody. He loved doing experiments, but he wasn't sure he wanted to do one with Ethan.

"We can dig another hole next to that one and put in some more seeds and then get some real fertilizer and see which one grows the fastest. Then we can tell which works the best, the fish or the fertilizer."

Woody had never heard Ethan say so much so fast. Or come up with such a good idea.

"We don't have any fertilizer," Woody said. "My mom used it."

"We do," said Ethan. "We could use some of ours."

Woody looked at him. Ethan had a kind of goofy smile on his face that went up on one side and down on the other.

Woody had never seen him smile before. He looked happy.

Woody suddenly realized that Ethan usually looked sad.

"Okay," Woody said. He followed Ethan across the street and up his driveway.

When Ethan opened the garage door, Woody couldn't believe his eyes. There was a lawn mower, a garbage can, and a small plastic bag.

Nothing else.

"You should see *our* garage," he said. "It's a mess."

It was. The Baldwins' garage was meant for

two cars. But there was only room for one. The rest had hammers and nails and potting soil and pots and hoses and rakes and pieces of wood all over the place.

Woody had his own workbench. It had hooks where he hung his hammer and screwdriver and saw. There was a cup for nails.

Every Saturday, he and his dad hammered and sawed and glued and painted. They transplanted seedlings. They made traps.

They never had to clean up. All Woody's mom said was, "One of these days I'm going to put a 'Yard Sale' sign in the front yard and get rid of all this junk."

"Don't you dare," his dad always said. "We're working on something."

They were. They never ran out of projects. Being in that garage made Woody feel good. He knew his dad felt the same way.

Being in Ethan's garage made him feel bad.

Ethan picked up the bag. They went back across the street and dug another hole. Ethan put in fertilizer and some seeds. Then he smoothed it over.

"We better label them," said Woody. He went into the house and came back with two slips of paper, a pen, and a roll of tape. He wrote "Huey" on one slip and taped it to his stick.

Ethan wrote "Other."

"I don't want to put 'Ethan,'" he said. "That'd make me feel like I'm in there." He stuck his stick in the ground.

"Want to see our garage?" said Woody.

"Sure."

"Follow me."

Woody ran into the garage with Ethan at his heels.

"Wow." Ethan smacked his forehead with his hand. He gave a long, two-note whistle. It sounded like "Oh, boy."

"You better clean this mess up, fast," he said. "Your mom's going to kill you."

"It's okay. It always looks like this," Woody said. "Do that again."

Ethan whistled.

"How'd you do that?" said Woody.

"It's easy," Ethan said. "You put your tongue behind your teeth like this." He tilted his head back and opened his mouth so Woody could see. "Then, you make your lips into slits." He made his lips flat with a little space between them.

"Then, you blow." He whistled again. Woody did all the things Ethan said, then blew. All that came out was air.

"You have to practice a lot," Ethan said. "My dad taught it to me. It's our family whistle. In case I get lost in stores and stuff." He came and stood by Woody's side at his workbench. "What are you making?"

"A bird feeder," said Woody. "I designed it myself."

He held up a square piece of plywood. It had a tin roof held up by four sticks. Under the roof was a wooden table with little stumps around it for chairs.

"It looks more like a bird restaurant," said

Ethan. "I wish I could make one. My dad loves birds."

"You can," said Woody. "My dad found lots of tin at the dump, and we have plenty of wood. I'll show you."

He got Ethan a hammer and showed him how to pound the tin until it was flat. While Ethan cut four sticks, Woody looked for the glue.

"My dad doesn't have a yard, but he can hang this on his balcony," said Ethan.

"Where does he live?" said Woody.

"In an apartment."

"Oh."

"It's really great. When I stay with him, he lets me rent movies and stay up till eleven o'clock and eat anything I want."

"Eleven o'clock?" Woody said.

Ethan nodded. "Yeah, and we play miniature golf and go to the movies and everything." He stopped sawing. "And you know what?"

"What?"

"Next weekend he's taking me to this big

hotel. It has an elevator and you can get food delivered to your room and he said I can buy soda in a machine and jump on the beds."

"Boy," said Woody, "you're lucky."

"Yeah." Ethan sawed another stick. When he spoke again, his voice sounded different. "Sometimes I kind of wish we could stay home and do nothing."

"Why don't you tell him?" said Woody.

"I don't know," Ethan shrugged his old shrug. "He might get mad or something. He might not want me to come over anymore."

"What do you mean?" Woody was amazed. "He's your dad."

Ethan didn't say anything. His arms were hanging at his sides. His head was hanging, too.

He reminded Woody of a puppet whose strings have been let go.

It was suddenly very quiet in the garage.

"You know what?" Woody said in a loud voice. Ethan didn't answer. "I got in such big trouble today, you wouldn't believe it."

Ethan looked at him. "How?"

Woody told him about Mrs. Carver and Miss Plunkett and show and tell and Huey. "Then she threw Huey into the garbage."

"What did you do?" said Ethan.

"I told her she stinks."

"You said that?"

"Yep."

"I can't believe it," Ethan said. His eyes were huge.

Now that Woody had told someone, he couldn't believe it, either. They stared at each other. When Mrs. Baldwin opened the door, they both jumped.

"What are you two up to?" she asked.

"Nothing, Mom." Woody picked up a hammer and started pounding. So did Ethan. "We're just working on something."

"Something tells me you're up to no good," Mrs. Baldwin said. But she was smiling. "Ethan, your mother's home, dear."

"Do I have to go now?" Ethan said. "I'm not done."

"Yeah, Mom, we're busy," said Woody.

"It's all right with me," she said. "I'll tell your mother you'll be home in a while."

She closed the door.

"What happened then?" Ethan said.

Woody told him.

"Boy, if I did that in my school, I'd be in big trouble," Ethan said.

"Yeah, it's a good thing she's new," Woody said. "I don't think she knows about the principal's office yet."

"She must hate you," Ethan said in an awed voice.

"No way." Woody was shocked. "Teachers can't hate children."

"Why not?" Ethan said.

"Because they can't, that's all," said Woody. "I think it's against the law."

"It is?"

Woody nodded.

"Well, I bet she's mad at you," said Ethan. "And when grownups get mad, they can do whatever they want. Especially to kids."

"Not teachers," Woody said stubbornly. "They have rules."

"They do?" Ethan said. "Like what?"

"If you're good, they have to give you a star," Woody said, "and if you're bad, they have to send you to time-out." The more he talked, the better he felt. "What do you think, they can send you to your room like your mom and dad?"

It sounded so silly, Ethan laughed. "Yeah, or take away your allowance?"

They started to work again.

But Woody was worried. He had been so mad at Miss Plunkett, he never thought about her being mad at him. He hated it when grownups got mad at him. All the good feeling seemed to leave the air. He felt as if he were all alone.

He swallowed. All he had said to Miss Plunkett was *stink*. That wasn't a swear word. Maybe she would forget by Monday.

Maybe Ethan was wrong.

Woody wasn't sure, but he hoped so.

6.

Miss Plunkett's Revenge

But Ethan was right.

Miss Plunkett *was* mad at him. All week long, whenever she was in charge, she was mean to him when he didn't even do anything.

On Monday, when he was line leader, she made him go to the back of the line.

"We weren't fighting, we were wrestling," he told her.

"Yeah," said Billy.

"I spoke to you two times, Woody," Miss Plunkett said. "That is no way for a line leader to act." She pointed to the end of the line. "Go."

On Wednesday, she made him almost die of thirst after recess.

"But I didn't get any," he said as she led him away from the water fountain.

"That's because you and Billy were too busy squirting it all over each other," she said. "Next time, aim for your mouth."

But Friday was the worst. On Friday, she told him he couldn't sit next to Billy for a week.

And he hadn't even done anything.

Jeremy had.

He was the one who made the rude noise during silent reading. Everyone knew it was him.

He always did it. Mrs. Carver would let them laugh a little, then tell them to go back to their work.

It wasn't even that funny anymore.

But with Miss Plunkett, it was.

When she heard the noise, she looked up from her book and said, "Did someone say something?"

That was funnier than what Jeremy did. They all started laughing.

"That's enough," Miss Plunkett said.

But they couldn't stop. Even Brianna. It was impossible to hold her nose and fold her hands at the same time.

Miss Plunkett stood up and came around from behind her desk.

Brianna ran over and whispered in her ear.

"Oh, I see." Miss Plunkett waited for a minute. Then she said, "That's enough," again in a louder voice.

It took a while, but they finally stopped.

Then Miss Plunkett ruined it. She cleared her throat and clasped her hands in front of her.

"Anyone who needs to pass gas should go out into the hall," she said in a polite voice.

Billy's eyebrows shot up under his bangs. "Pass gas?" he said in a high voice.

It was the most embarrassing thing they had ever heard. The boys shrieked. The girls got bright red and clamped their hands over their mouths.

Woody laughed so hard, he fell off his chair.

It didn't feel as if they'd ever be able to stop.

Until Miss Plunkett turned off the lights.

When a teacher turned off the lights, it meant you had better stop what you were doing. Or else.

When Miss Plunkett turned them back on, her mouth was an angry red slash across her face.

"I want everyone sitting on their bottoms in circle. Now," she said. Her voice was low and kind of shaky.

They skittered sideways like crabs into circle.

Miss Plunkett went behind the desk and blew her nose.

"I don't know why it's called the bottom. It's really the middle," Billy whispered. "It would only be the bottom if your hands and feet were up in the air. Like this."

He leaned back and put his hands in the air. He lifted both feet off the floor. For a second he balanced. Then he fell over on top of Woody.

Woody fell on top of Andrew, who fell on top of Lynn.

"Miss Plunkett," Lynn wailed.

Billy ended up out in the hall. Woody ended up at a table by himself.

Miss Plunkett said they couldn't sit together for a whole week.

"She can't do that," Billy said. They were walking toward the buses. "Let's tell Mrs. Carver."

"She won't do anything," Woody said bitterly. He remembered Huey. "She's on Miss Plunkett's side."

"Yeah," Billy said. "The enemy side, right?"

"Right."

Woody thought about it all the way home.

Not the part about Mrs. Carver being an enemy. He didn't like to think about that part.

The part about Miss Plunkett. About how she thought a rude noise was someone talking. How she said something ridiculous like "pass gas," then expected them not to laugh.

He could hardly wait to tell Ethan.

He opened the kitchen door and dropped his backpack on the floor. "Hi, Mom. Where's Ethan?"

"Hang that on a hook, Woody." His mom kissed him. "Ethan isn't here yet. Don't you want a snack? I made sugar cookies."

"I'm not really hungry." Woody hung up his pack and went over to the sink. He pushed himself up so he could see over the windowsill. Ethan was sitting on his front stoop. "He's on the steps. Can I go over? I want to tell him something."

"Okay," said his mom. "Make sure you look both ways."

Woody let the screen door slam behind him.

"Hey, Ethan!" Woody stopped at the end of his driveway. He looked to the left, then to the right. Then he raced across the street.

"Want to hear something?" Woody asked. He sat down on the top step. Ethan didn't look up.

"It's really funny. You want to hear?"

Ethan shrugged. "I don't care." He had his elbows on his knees and his chin in his hands. He was staring at the empty street.

"What's wrong with you?" said Woody.

Ethan shrugged again.

Woody watched him for a minute, but Ethan wouldn't look at him. "You want to come over?"

"I don't care."

"What do you mean?" said Woody. "You want to give your dad the bird restaurant when you go to his apartment, don't you?"

"I'm not going. He has a business trip."

"You mean, you're not going to the hotel?"

Ethan shook his head.

"Oh." Woody thought for a minute. "Well, maybe you will next weekend."

"I won't see him next weekend. My mom says if he misses his turn, it's his fault."

"Oh." Woody had never heard about parents taking turns.

"I won't see him for two weeks," Ethan said. "Two whole weeks."

Woody blinked. He saw his dad every night. And every morning. He couldn't imagine not seeing him for two weeks. He wouldn't get to kiss him good night. Or sit in his lap. He might worry his dad didn't love him anymore.

It would make him feel terrible.

It would make him feel like crying.

He looked at Ethan's face, then at the ground.

"I told you grownups were mean," Ethan said in a small voice.

"Maybe you should tell him how much you want to go," Woody said. "You could call him at work."

"I don't know his number," Ethan said.

"You don't?" Woody knew his dad's number by heart. 555-8988.

He didn't know what to say to a kid who didn't know his own dad's phone number.

He put his chin down on his hands. He felt terrible. If Ethan started to cry, he knew he might, too. The thought made him so nervous, he jumped to his feet.

"I know," Woody said. He pulled at his eyebrow. "You can spend the night at my house. We can finish the bird restaurant and put up my tent and eat popcorn and everything."

Ethan didn't say anything.

"It'll be great, Ethan, really. Maybe my dad will take us to play miniature golf."

Ethan looked up. "You think he would?"

"Sure." Woody felt so glad, he couldn't stay still. "I'll go ask my mom."

He ran home as fast as he could and found his mom in the living room.

"We have to ask his mother, but it's okay with me," Mrs. Baldwin said. Woody squeezed her around her waist.

"Hey, what's up?" she said, laughing. But Woody was gone. He ran back across the road.

Ethan's front steps were empty. The front door was wide open.

"My mom said yes," Woody shouted. He stuck his head in the door.

Ethan was on the phone. "Sure. Okay. Great. I love you, too."

He slammed down the phone and whirled around. "That was my dad! He canceled his trip till next week. He said being with me was more important than any darn old business trip."

His face was shining as if a flashlight had gone on inside his head.

"I get to stay till Monday. He's picking me up after work." Ethan's voice got worried. "Do you think I can finish my restaurant by then?"

"Sure," Woody said. "Last one there's a rotten egg."

They raced each other back across the street.

Woody took a giant leap and tried to grab the lowest branch of the maple tree in his front yard.

Of course Ethan's dad loved him, Woody thought. Just because he didn't live with Ethan didn't mean anything.

Dads loved their sons, no matter what.

Woody already knew that, but it felt good to make sure.

7.

The Greatest Worm

"**H**ey, Woody!"

Billy came up behind Woody and grabbed his backpack. "Wait until you see what I got this weekend. The greatest worm."

Woody and Billy both liked worms. Especially dead, dry ones. They were making a collection together. Sometimes they looked for them on the playground during recess.

They crouched down against the wall outside their classroom. Billy started pulling everything out of his pack.

The last bell rang.

"Hurry up," Woody said. "We're going to get in trouble."

"Hold on a minute. You've got to see this."

"You're late." Brianna was standing by the door with her hands on her hips.

Billy pulled out a small paper bag. "Here it is."

"I'm telling," Brianna said. They ignored her. She spun around and went into the room.

"It's the greatest one we've ever found," Billy said. He turned the bag upside down. A long squashed worm dropped into Woody's hand. It was about six inches long and as straight as a pencil.

"I found it on the way to the bus," Billy said. "Isn't it cool?"

"Yeah," Woody said. "It's the star, all right."

"Excuse me."

Miss Plunkett was standing in the doorway. Brianna was behind her. Woody closed his hand over the worm.

"That was the last bell," Miss Plunkett said.

"They're doing something disgusting," said Brianna. "I saw."

"Stand up, please," Miss Plunkett said. "What's in your hand, Woody?"

Woody put his hand behind his back. "Nothing."

"Let me see it."

Woody shook his head. "You won't like it."

"Let me see it." Miss Plunkett held out her hand.

Woody brought his hand from behind his back and looked at his fist. He looked at Miss Plunkett's face.

"Now," she said.

He clamped his lips together, opened his hand, and dropped the worm into Miss Plunkett's hand.

For a second she stared at it. Then she snatched her hand back as if something had bitten her. The worm fell to the floor.

"Watch out!" Billy said. "You'll break it." He ducked down to pick it up.

"Leave it there," Miss Plunkett said. She was

wiping her hand furiously with her handker-
chief.

"But—"

"I said, leave it there."

"I told you it was disgusting," Brianna said.

"Go back to your seat, Brianna," Miss Plunkett
said. "This is none of your business."

Brianna looked shocked, then hurt. She
glared at them with mean, slitty eyes.

Woody smirked.

"You think this is funny, Woody?" Miss
Plunkett said.

"No."

She looked from one boy to the other. "I want
you two to go down to the principal's office
right now."

"I told you—" Woody began.

"*Now.*"

Woody grabbed Billy's sleeve. "Come on." He
recognized her quiet voice. He thought they'd
be safer in the principal's office.

Anywhere but here.

◆ ◆ ◆

Mrs. Cheek, the school secretary, frowned at them over the top of her glasses. "Mr. Grant is busy. You'll have to wait."

She didn't know the story, but Woody could tell she already thought they were guilty.

"You," she said to Billy, "sit over there."

"And you," to Woody, "take a seat over there." She pointed to the opposite side of the room. "And no talking."

She went back to her work.

Billy threw himself into his chair and kicked the leg.

"No kicking, either," Mrs. Cheek said. She didn't look up.

They heard morning announcements over the loudspeaker. Kids kept coming into the office and out again. The younger kids stared at them as if they were criminals. The older kids put their hands over their mouths and made laughing motions.

A fifth-grader named Brad drew his finger

across his neck, like they were going to have their heads cut off.

Woody slid down in his seat. This was the first time he had been sent to the principal's office. He didn't know what would happen. He was scared, but he was mad, too.

He had tried to tell Miss Plunkett, but she wouldn't listen. He crossed his arms over his chest.

"I'd work at having a better attitude if I were you, Woody," Mrs. Cheek said. "You're in trouble as it is."

Woody narrowed his eyes at the calendar on the wall behind her.

Suddenly, Mr. Grant's door opened. He came out with one arm halfway in his jacket sleeve, the other hand holding a briefcase.

"I have to go to the superintendent's office for a meeting," he told Mrs. Cheek. "I shouldn't be more than an hour."

She nodded in their direction. "What do you want to do about them?"

"Woody. Billy," said Mr. Grant. "What are you

two doing here first thing Monday morning?"

"I was just showing him something," Billy muttered.

"It was a worm," said Woody. "I told Miss Plunkett she wouldn't like it."

"A worm, huh?" Mr. Grant shook his head. "That's a ticklish area, boys. There are people who like them and people who don't."

"It wasn't alive," said Billy.

"That doesn't seem to make any difference when it comes to worms, Billy," Mr. Grant said. "In the future, I suggest you either keep them outside or on the end of a hook, okay?"

The boys nodded.

"Okay, go back to class and work hard." Mr. Grant went to the door and held it open.

Woody stood up. He couldn't believe it.

Mr. Grant wasn't mad. They weren't in trouble.

It was over.

He felt as if he couldn't get out of there fast enough.

He and Billy reached the door at the same

time. Billy stepped on the back of his sneaker. Woody almost fell.

They didn't stop until they made it around the corner. Then Billy fell against the wall.

Woody knelt down to fix his sneaker. His heart was racing. He felt the way he felt on a roller coaster—thrilled and sick at the same time.

It was as if he had escaped from jail. He was free. But he needed to find cover, fast.

He stood up. "Come on," he said. They started down the hall. Then Billy grabbed his arm.

"Look."

He pointed. Halfway down the hall, in the middle of the floor, was a pair of shoes. Red high heels, sitting side by side.

Nobody was in them.

Woody didn't know why, but two shoes in the middle of an empty hall without a person in them seemed like the funniest thing he had ever seen.

He clamped his hand over his mouth and

crouched down behind Billy. They tiptoed closer. Suddenly, Billy put his arm out and hit Woody across the chest.

Someone was humming. Someone very close.

Woody looked to the right. It was Miss Plunkett. She was standing up in the art display case, pinning a picture to the wall. Her back was to them.

Her feet were bare.

Woody couldn't take his eyes off her. He couldn't move.

Billy could. Without a word, he darted forward, grabbed the shoes, and took off down the hall.

It was over in a second.

Woody didn't want to run, but he didn't want to stay. If he was there when Miss Plunkett turned around, he was dead.

He ran. Past the display case, past the art room door, down to the end of the hall as fast as he could go on tiptoe.

Billy was standing next to a garbage can. When

Woody came up to him, he held the shoes up in the air.

"What are you going to do?" Woody whispered.

Billy grinned. Then he pushed in the swinging lid and dropped the shoes into the can.

Billy had thrown away Miss Plunkett's shoes!

Woody was sure his heart was going to jump out of his mouth and end up on the floor. He looked from Billy's empty hands to the garbage can. Maybe he could get them out of there. Maybe he could do it before anyone saw him.

He put his hand on the lid.

"Where are you boys supposed to be?"

Woody spun around. Billy jumped back and knocked into the can.

Ms. Stamp, the gym teacher, was standing in front of them.

"Class," said Woody.

"Well, then, get there," she said.

Woody could feel her eyes on his back all the way down the hall. He didn't dare look at Billy.

"You're crazy," Woody whispered out of the side of his mouth.

"You did it, too."

"I did not."

"Did, too."

"Boys?" Ms. Stamp's warning voice came down the hall.

They didn't say another word until they got to their room. Woody put his hand on the doorknob.

"We've got to get them back," he said.

"No way," said Billy. "I'm not getting in more trouble."

Woody didn't say anything. But he knew he had to think of something.

Facing Miss Plunkett was going to be hard enough.

Facing a barefoot Miss Plunkett would be impossible.

8.

Things to Remember

Mrs. Carver was waiting for them.
"Miss Plunkett told me about this morning."

They were standing in front of her desk. She looked from one to the other. "I've just about had it with you two."

Her voice was very low. "I don't know what has gotten into you. You have done nothing but disrupt my class since last week."

Woody felt as if her eyes were boring holes into his brain. He hoped she couldn't see what was written there.

"One more incident and I'm calling your parents, Woody."

He swallowed.

"And your grandmother, Billy. Do you both understand?"

They nodded. Mrs. Carver stared at them for another minute. Then she said, "Everyone is working on the story Miss Plunkett assigned. Get to work."

Woody went to his desk and took out his journal. He opened it to the page with the picture of Huey on top.

He stared at it without seeing it.

He couldn't write about fish right now. He couldn't even think about them. He was waiting for the door to open. For Miss Plunkett to come in.

He wouldn't have to say anything. All she would have to do was look at him to know he was guilty.

But the door didn't open. All the kids were hunched over their desks, writing. Woody pretended he was thinking, but he couldn't. He needed to move. He needed to tell someone.

He needed to get the shoes.

He stood up and walked to Mrs. Carver's desk. "I have to go to the bathroom," he said in a low voice.

She held out the pass to the boys' room. "Come right back."

There was no one in the hall. Woody walked past the boys' room and the water fountain. When he got to the door of the conference room, he saw something out of the corner of his eye.

Miss Plunkett was sitting at the table. She looked at him without smiling.

"Hi," Woody said.

"Hi."

That was all. Woody waited to see what she would say next. Miss Plunkett held her feet up off the floor in front of her and wiggled her toes. "My shoes seem to have walked away without me." She tried to make it sound as if it were funny.

Woody stared at her bare feet.

"I know where they are," he said.

"You do?"

He nodded.

"Would you get them for me?"

"I'll be right back."

He ran to the garbage can and pushed in the lid. The shoes were sitting on top. He picked them up and hurried back to the conference room.

The moment she saw them, Miss Plunkett gave the biggest sigh he had ever heard. "Oh, thank you, Woody." She put them on the floor and slipped her feet into them. "I can't tell you how awful I felt without them. It was terrible. I didn't know what I was going to say to Mr. Grant if he saw me. Not many people walk around the school barefoot, do they?"

"They'd probably like to," Woody said, "but it would get too smelly."

Miss Plunkett laughed. She sounded so pleased, Woody smiled. "Yes, it probably would.

"Well." She took one last look at her feet. "Mrs. Carver must be wondering what happened to me. Come on." Woody walked beside her down the hall.

Miss Plunkett started talking. "You know what I was thinking about while I was sitting in the conference room? A girl named Patty Clark. She was in my class when I was your age. She came from a very poor family. She must have had seven or eight brothers and sisters. They lived at the end of a long dirt road in a house made of cement blocks.

"I can still picture it." She looked down at him. "Patty's hair was always dirty and her clothes were always way too big for her. No one wanted to sit next to her in class."

She stopped walking because they were near their room. "One day, we were playing kickball. It was very muddy and there was this one big puddle our teacher told us to stay away from. But when Alan Jacobs kicked the ball into it, Patty went right after it. Her shoes were so big, they got stuck in the mud and came off.

"She didn't have socks on and her shoes were filled with mud. Mrs. Nichols was so mad."

"Why was she mad?" said Woody. "They weren't *her* shoes."

"No, but she'd said to stay out of the mud and Patty didn't listen. I guess she felt responsible. Anyway, she made Patty walk back into the school in her bare feet.

"And you know what we did?"

"What?" Woody said.

"We laughed at her. We all stood around and laughed while she walked down the hall, crying."

Woody didn't know if he felt more terrible for Patty Clark or Miss Plunkett. That's how sad she sounded.

They walked to the door without talking. "Now I know how she felt, Woody. And it reminded me. You should always try to imagine how somebody feels before you laugh at them or judge them. Do you know what I mean?"

Woody thought about Ethan. "Kind of."

"You try to remember that, okay?"

"Okay."

"Good boy." A big, friendly smile broke out on her face. "We'd better get to work, or Mrs. Carver will make us miss recess."

She made a funny face and Woody grinned. He went in, sat down at his desk, and turned over his journal.

He knew he could write about Huey now. He felt proud Miss Plunkett had told him about Patty. He would try to remember it, like she said.

There was another thing about Miss Plunkett he definitely would remember.

About her and the shoes.

She didn't ask him where they were. And she didn't ask him how he knew.

Woody knew he would remember that for a long time.

9.

This Is Walter. He's Alive

"**H**ey, Woody, my dad!"

There was a green car in Ethan's driveway. He was standing next to it, waving. A tall, thin man was standing next to him. Woody went across the street.

Ethan's dad put out his hand. "Nice to meet you, Woody. Ethan's told me a lot about you."

Woody put out his left hand first, then his right. But Ethan's dad acted like he didn't notice. He shook Woody's hand very seriously. He looked just like Ethan, only taller. They had the same smile, which they were smiling now.

"I love my bird restaurant, Woody," Mr. Adams said. "Thank you for helping Ethan with it. I can see why he says you're his best friend."

"He does?" Woody looked at Ethan, who ducked his head.

Woody thought about Billy. How they always got into trouble. How Billy deserted him about the shoes.

"He's mine, too," he told Ethan's dad. Ethan looked up and smiled his goofy smile.

"Well, you're lucky to have each other, that's all I can say." Ethan's dad leaned down and kissed Ethan on the top of the head. Ethan reached up to hug him. "I have to go now, Eth. Maybe the weekend after next when we get together and do nothing, Woody would like to come."

"Yeah. My dad could teach you our whistle," said Ethan.

"That would be great," said Woody.

They watched Mr. Adams's car as it disappeared around the corner. They heard him honk.

"I did what you said. I told my dad I didn't want to go anywhere, I just wanted to sit around," Ethan said as they walked up Woody's driveway. "It was great. I told him about your garage and our experiment and everything. He says we have to record what happens every day."

They walked over to the two sticks and knelt down. Nothing was growing. Ethan scratched his head. "That's funny."

"What's funny?" said Mrs. Baldwin. She was holding a basket of clean laundry.

"We took some seeds from the kitchen drawer and planted them, but nothing's happening," said Woody.

"Oh, those," Mrs. Baldwin said. "I wouldn't hold out too much hope for those. Those seeds have been in that drawer since before you were born, Woody. I hated to throw them out."

"Great, Mom," Woody said. "Good thing

Ethan's dad doesn't have you for an assistant."

"Yeah," agreed Ethan. "You'd get fired."

"Darn." Mrs. Baldwin snapped her fingers. "Another job opportunity down the drain. I guess I'd better stick to being your mother."

"It's not funny, Mom," Woody said. "Come on, Ethan."

He led Ethan over to the back fence. "This is the greatest place to find salamanders." Woody crouched down and started to turn over rocks.

"She's not so bad," he said suddenly.

"Who?" said Ethan.

"Miss Plunkett."

"What do you mean?" said Ethan. "You hate her."

"Not anymore," Woody said. He told Ethan about the principal's office and the shoes and how Miss Plunkett didn't ask where they came from.

He didn't tell him about Patty Clark. That was a secret between him and Miss Plunkett.

"You sure are lucky," Ethan said. "You could

have been in big trouble. That guy Billy is crazy."

"Yeah." It made Woody shiver, thinking about it. Tomorrow, he would tell Billy he already had a best friend. He would go back to being regular Woody Baldwin. Mrs. Carver would think he was a Good Citizen again.

He could hardly wait.

He turned over a rock and saw a flash of something dark. He lunged toward it.

"Got it." He held up a long, squiggling thing in his hand.

"Wow. That's the biggest worm I've ever seen," said Ethan.

"It's not a worm, it's a worm snake," said Woody. It was writhing back and forth in his hand. It kept curling its long, skinny body around his fingers.

"You better watch out," Ethan said. "I bet he bites."

"All snakes can bite, but this guy won't," Woody said. "Worm snakes are nice. You want to hold him?"

"No, thanks," Ethan said.

"Just touch him. He won't hurt you."

Ethan touched the skin of the snake with the tip of his pointer finger.

"His name is Walter," Woody said. "Walter Baldwin."

"Hey, he's smooth," Ethan said with surprise. He touched him again. "Hi, Walter."

"Come on, I've got to make a home for him." Woody stood up. "I'm going to take him to show and tell."

"You better not," Ethan said. He followed Woody into the garage. "Miss Plunkett hates animals, remember?"

"Only dead ones," Woody said. "She said she likes live ones. She'll love Walter."

"I don't know," Ethan said. "My mother hates snakes. She screams if she even sees a small one."

"Miss Plunkett's not like a mother," Woody said. "She's a teacher. Teachers don't scream at stuff like that."

Ethan was pretty smart, but he didn't know everything. He didn't know Miss Plunkett had told Woody something very important. Something she hadn't told the other kids.

Woody knew you didn't tell someone something important unless you liked them.

By showing her Walter, Woody could let Miss Plunkett know he liked her back.

He would put Walter in a box.

When it was his turn, he would take Walter out and hold him up in the air.

He would say, "This is Walter. He's alive."

He could hardly wait to see Miss Plunkett's face.

He could hardly wait for show and tell.

Stephanie Greene

was born in New York City, the middle child of
five, and grew up in Connecticut. She has
worked as a newspaper reporter, an advertising
copywriter, and a creative director. She lives in
Chapel Hill, North Carolina, with her husband
and their son Oliver. Ms. Greene is the daughter
of Constance C. Greene, the acclaimed children's novelist, and is the author of *Owen Foote,
Soccer Star* and *Owen Foote, Second Grade
Strongman.*

Elaine Clayton

is the illustrator of *Five Alien Elves* and *Six
Haunted Hairdos* by Gregory Maguire, and *The
Boy with Dinosaur Hands* by Al Carusone. She
also writes and illustrates picture books for
young children. Ms. Clayton lives with her family in New Jersey.

Stephanie Greene

was born in New York City, the middle child of five, and grew up in Connecticut. She has worked as a newspaper reporter, an advertising copywriter, and a creative director. She lives in Chapel Hill, North Carolina, with her husband and their son Oliver. Ms. Greene is the daughter of Constance C. Greene, the acclaimed children's novelist, and is the author of *Owen Foote, Soccer Star* and *Owen Foote, Second Grade Strongman.*

Elaine Clayton

is the illustrator of *Five Alien Elves* and *Six Haunted Hairdos* by Gregory Maguire, and *The Boy with Dinosaur Hands* by Al Carusone. She also writes and illustrates picture books for young children. Ms. Clayton lives with her family in New Jersey.